𝔚illiam 𝔖hakespeare's

The Tempest

EDITED BY
Philip Page and Marilyn Pettit

ILLUSTRATED BY
Philip Page

Published in association with

Hodder Murray

A MEMBER OF THE HODDER HEADLINE GROUP

Orders: please contact Bookpoint Ltd, 130 Milton Park, Abingdon, Oxon OX14 4SB.
Telephone: (44) 01235 827720. Fax: (44) 01235 400454. Lines are open 9.00–6.00, Monday
to Saturday, with a 24-hour message answering service. Visit our website at
www.hoddereducation.co.uk

A catalogue record for this title is available from the British Library.

First published in 2006 by
Hodder Murray, a member of the Hodder Headline Group
338 Euston Road
London NW1 3BH

Impression number   10 9 8 7 6 5 4 3 2 1
Year   2011 2010 2009 2008 2007 2006

Cover illustration by Taxi/Getty Images
Typeset by DC Graphic Design Limited, Swanley, Kent
Printed in Great Britain by Martins the Printers, Berwick upon Tweed

Papers used in this book are natural, renewable and recyclable products. They are made from
wood grown in sustainable forests. The logging and manufacturing processes conform to the
environmental regulations of the country of origin.

ISBN-10: 0340 88814 8
ISBN-13: 978 0340 88814 8

Contents

About the play

The Tempest has something for everyone! It has:

magic and mystery
plots to murder
drunken foolishness
music, dance, masque
and a love story.

There are also dark sides to this play:

Prospero's treatment of Caliban
Caliban's attempted rape of Miranda.

As well as all these ingredients, Shakespeare encourages us to learn lessons from the play. As you read, decide what these lessons might be. Share your ideas with your group as you work through the text.

One, relating to Prospero in particular, might make you very happy, especially if you share it with your teacher!

Cast of characters

Alonso
King of Naples

Ferdinand
Alonso's son

Sebastian
Alonso's brother

Prospero
The rightful Duke of Milan

Miranda
Prospero's daughter

Antonio
Prospero's brother and
Duke of Milan

Ariel

Caliban
Prospero's servants

Gonzalo
Alonso's adviser

Trinculo
A jester

Stephano
A drunken butler

Adrian   **Francisco**
Noblemen

Master   **Boatswain**
Sailors

Iris
Juno's messenger

Juno
Queen of Heaven

Ceres
Goddess of Fertility

Spirits called by Prospero's magic

The ship carrying Alonso, the King of Naples, is wrecked in a terrible storm.

> **Boatswain**! Speak to th' mariners. Fall to't **yarely** or we run ourselves aground.

Boatswain – (pronounced 'bosun') ship's officer in charge of the sails
yarely – quickly

You do assist the storm. – You're getting in the way.

A plague upon this howling. **They** are louder than the weather or our **office**.

Again? What do you here?

A pox o' your throat, you bawling dog!

Work you, then.

Hang, cur! You insolent noise-maker!

Let's assist them.

I'm out of patience.

We split, we split, we split!

Let's all sink wi' th' King.

Let's take leave of him.

Now would I give a thousand **furlongs** of sea for an acre of barren ground. I would **fain** die a dry death.

They – the passengers   **office** – work
furlong – 220 yards (about 200m)   **fain** – gladly

Prospero stops the storm he created and explains to Miranda how they came to the island.

If by your **art**, my dearest father, you have put the wild waters in this roar, allay them.

I saw a brave vessel (who no doubt had some noble creature in her) dashed all to pieces.

Lend thy hand and pluck my magic garment from me.

I have safely ordered that there is no soul – no, not so much **perdition** as an hair, **betid** to any creature in the vessel.

Sit down, for thou must now know further.

You have often begun to tell me what I am, but stopped.

art – magic
perdition – loss
betid – happened

cell – simple home   manage – management   absolute Milan – the only ruler of Milan
So dry he was for sway – So ambitious he was for power

Prospero: This King of Naples, being an enemy
To me inveterate, hearkens my brother's suit,
Which was that he, in lieu o' th' premises
Of homage, and I know not how much **tribute**,   money
Should presently **extirpate** me and mine   destroy
Out of the dukedom, and confer fair Milan,
With all the honours, on my brother. Whereon –
A treacherous army **levied** – one midnight   gathered
Fated to th' purpose, did Antonio open
The gates of Milan and i' th' dead of darkness
The ministers for th' purpose hurried thence
Me and thy crying self.

Miranda: I, not rememb'ring how I cried out then,
Will cry it o'er again. It is a hint
That wrings mine eyes to't.

Prospero: Hear a little further,
And then I'll bring thee to the present business
Which now's upon's, without the which this story
Were **most impertinent**.   pointless

Miranda: Wherefore did they not that hour destroy us?

Prospero: They durst not, so dear the love my people
   bore me.
They hurried us aboard a **bark**,   ship
Bore us some leagues to sea, where they prepared
A rotten carcass of a **butt**, not rigged,   small boat
Nor tackle, sail nor mast – the very rats
Instinctively have quit it. There they hoist us
To cry to th' sea, that roared to us.

Miranda: What trouble was I then to you?

Prospero: Thou wast that did preserve me.

Miranda: How came we ashore?

Prospero: Some food we had, and some fresh water, that
A noble Neapolitan, Gonzalo,
Out of his charity did give us, with
Rich garments, linens, stuffs and necessaries.
Knowing I loved my books, he furnished me
From mine own library with volumes that
I prize above my dukedom

Miranda: Would I might see that man!

Prospero: Here in this island we arrived, and here
Have I, thy schoolmaster, **made thee more profit**   taught you better
Than other princes can.

Miranda: And now I pray you, sir, your reason
For raising this sea-storm?

Prospero: By accident most strange, fortune hath mine
     enemies
Brought to this shore.
Cease more questions, thou art inclined to sleep.

> # Think about it
>
> What kind of life has Miranda had up to this
> point?

Prospero summons the spirit Ariel, who asks for his freedom. Prospero reminds him of the debt the spirit owes him!

I am ready now. Approach, my Ariel. Come.

All hail, great master! I come to answer thy best pleasure.

Hast thou, spirit, performed **to point** the tempest that I **bade** thee?

I boarded the King's ship; on the deck, in every cabin I flamed amazement.

Who was so firm, that this **coil** would not affect his reason?

Not a soul but felt a fever of the mad.

But are they safe?

Not a hair perished.

to point – exactly   **bade** – commanded
coil – confusion

In troops I have dispersed them 'bout the isle. The King's son have I landed by himself, whom I left sitting, his arms **in this sad knot**.

And the rest o' th' fleet?

Safely in harbour. The mariners with a charm I have left asleep. The rest o' th' fleet have met again, and are bound sadly home for Naples, supposing that they saw the King's ship wrecked and his great person perish.

Thy charge is performed; but there's more work.

Let me **remember** thee what thou hast promised.

What is't thou canst demand?

My liberty.

Before thy time be out? No more!

I have done thee worthy service. Thou did promise to **bate** me a full year.

Dost thou forget from what a torment I did free thee?

Hast thou forgot the foul witch Sycorax?

No, sir.

in this sad knot – folded   **remember** – remind
bate – reduce

9

This damned witch was brought with child, and here was left by th' sailors. Thou, my slave, was then her servant.

Thou wast a spirit too delicate to act her commands, refusing her – she did confine thee into a **cloven** pine, imprisoned a dozen years.

She died and left thee there. Then was this island (save for the son she did **litter** here) not honoured with a human shape.

Yes, Caliban, her son.

He, that Caliban whom now I keep in service.

It was mine art that made gape the pine and let thee out.

I thank thee, master.

If thou more murmur'st, I will **rend** an oak and peg thee in his knotty entrails till thou hast howled away twelve winters.

Pardon, master; I will do my spiriting **gently**.

Do so, and after two days I will discharge thee.

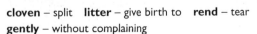

cloven – split **litter** – give birth to **rend** – tear
gently – without complaining

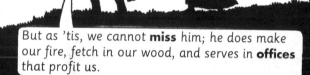

miss – do without
offices – duties

**Act 1
Scene 2**

Caliban complains about the way he is treated until Prospero threatens him with his magic.

Caliban: This island's mine by Sycorax my mother,
Which thou tak'st from me. When thou cam'st first
Thou strok'st me, and made much of me; wouldst give me
Water with berries in't, and teach me how
To name the **bigger light** and how **the less**   sun   moon
That burn by day and night. And then I loved thee,
And showed thee all the qualities o' th' isle:
The fresh springs, **brine** pits, barren place and fertile.   salt water
Cursed be I that did so! All the charms
Of Sycorax – toads, beetles, bats – light on you,
For I am all the subjects that you have,
Which first was mine own king; and here you sty me
In this hard rock, whiles you do keep from me
The rest o' th' island.

Prospero: Thou most lying slave,
Whom **stripes** may move, not kindness; I have used thee   whipping
(Filth as thou art) with humane care and lodged thee
In mine own cell, till thou didst seek to **violate**   rape
The honour of my child.

Caliban: O ho, O ho! Would't had been done;
Thou didst prevent me, I had peopled else
This isle with Calibans.

Miranda: Slave, I pitied thee,
Took pains to make thee speak, taught thee each hour
One thing or other. When thou didst not, savage,
Know thine own meaning, but wouldst gabble like
A thing most brutish, I endowed thy purposes
With words that made them known; but thy vile race,
(Though thou didst learn) had that in't which good natures
Could not abide to be with; therefore wast thou
Deservedly confined into this rock,
Who had deserved more than a prison.

Caliban: You taught me language, and my profit on't
Is I know how to curse. The red plague rid you
For learning me your language.

Prospero: Hag-seed, hence: Witch's child
Fetch us in fuel, and be quick – thou'rt best –
To answer other business. Shrug'st thou, malice?
If thou neglect'st, or dost unwillingly
What I command, I'll rack thee with old cramps,
Fill all thy bones with aches, make thee roar,
That beasts shall tremble at thy din.

Caliban: No, pray thee. I must obey; his art is of such
power.

Think about it

Who do you most feel sorry for in this
scene, and why?

Ariel leads Ferdinand to Prospero and Miranda. The two young people fall in love – a little too quickly for Prospero's liking!

Where should this music be?

I have followed it, or it hath drawn me.

It begins again. This is no mortal business.

Say what thou seest yond.

What is't? a spirit?

No, it eats, and sleeps and hath such senses as we have. This **gallant** was in the wreck.

I might call him a thing divine.

It goes on, I see.

gallant – young man
It goes on, I see. – My plan is working.

14

maid – a real young lady (not a goddess)   twain – two
changed eyes – fallen in love at first sight

usurp – take/seize   manacle – chain

16

I have no ambition to see a goodlier man.

My father's loss, the wreck of all my friends, nor this man's threats are but light to me, might I but through my prison once a day behold this maid.

It works. Thou hast done well, fine Ariel.

Be of comfort; my father's of a better nature, sir, than he appears by speech.

Thou shalt be free; but do all my command.

To th' syllable.

Come, follow.

Speak not for him.

On another part of the island Alonso thinks his son has drowned and a murder is planned.

Beseech you, sir, be merry. You have cause of joy, for our escape is much beyond our loss.

Prithee, peace.

Though this island seem to be **desert** – uninhabitable and almost inaccessible –

Yet –

Yet –

He could not miss't.

It must needs be of subtle, tender, and delicate temperance.

The air breathes upon us here most sweetly.

As if it had lungs, and rotten ones.

How lush and lusty the grass looks! How green!

The ground indeed is **tawny**.

With **an eye** of green in't.

Prithee – Please
desert – deserted
tawny – yellowy-brown

He could not miss't. – He can't stop talking about the island.
an eye – a touch/bit

Methinks our garments seem now as fresh as when we were at Tunis at the marriage of your daughter.

Would I had never married my daughter there, for coming thence my son is lost

O mine heir of Naples and of Milan, what strange fish hath made his meal on thee?

Sir, he may live. I saw him; he oared himself with his good arms to th' shore. I do not doubt he came alive to land.

No, no, he's gone.

Sir, you may thank yourself for this great loss, that would not bless our Europe with your daughter, but rather loose her to an African. The fault's your own.

My lord Sebastian, the truth you speak doth lack some gentleness, and time to speak it in.

Had I **plantation** of this isle, and were the king on't, what would I do?

No occupation, all men idle, all; and women too, but innocent and pure; no **sovereignty** – sword, pike, knife, gun, or need of any **engine** would I not have.

plantation – the job of settling
sovereignty – ruler
engine – machine

19

Nature should bring forth abundance to feed my innocent people.

Long live Gonzalo!

Your highness, these gentlemen laugh at nothing.

'Twas you we laughed at.

Will you laugh me asleep, for I am very heavy?

Go sleep.

What, all asleep? I wish mine eyes would shut up my thoughts.

We two, my lord, will guard your person while you rest, and watch your safety.

I find not myself disposed to sleep.

Nor I.

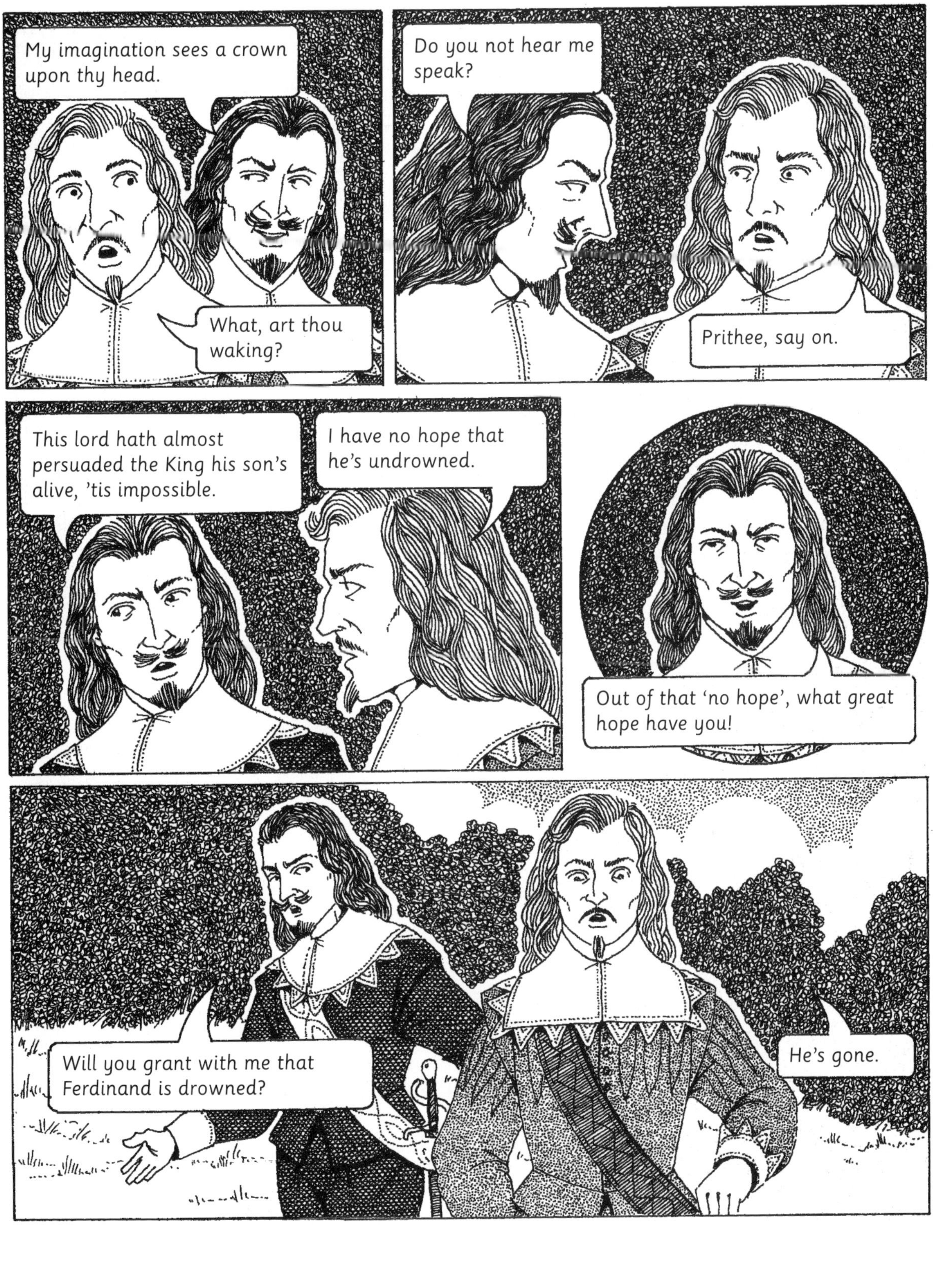
My imagination sees a crown upon thy head.
What, art thou waking?
Do you not hear me speak?
Prithee, say on.
This lord hath almost persuaded the King his son's alive, 'tis impossible.
I have no hope that he's undrowned.
Out of that 'no hope', what great hope have you!
Will you grant with me that Ferdinand is drowned?
He's gone.

Antonio: Then tell me, who's the next heir of Naples?

Sebastian: Claribel.

Antonio: She that is Queen of Tunis; she that dwells
Ten leagues beyond man's life; she that from Naples
Can have no note unless the sun **were post** –   brought the news
The man i' th' moon's too slow – till new-born chins
Be rough and razorable; she that from whom
We all were sea-swallowed, though some **cast** again,   saved
And by that destiny, to perform an act
Whereof what's past is **prologue**, what to come   an introduction
In yours and mine discharge!

Sebastian: How say you?
'Tis true my brother's daughter's Queen of Tunis,
So is she heir of Naples, 'twixt which regions
There is some space.

Antonio: A space whose every **cubit**   a measurement – about 50cm
Seems to cry out, 'How shall that Claribel
Measure us back to Naples? Keep in Tunis,
And let Sebastian wake.' Say this were death
That now hath seized them; why, they were no worse
Than now they are. What a sleep were this
For your advancement! Do you understand me?

Sebastian: Methinks I do. I remember
You did **supplant** your brother Prospero.   overthrow

Antonio: True: and look how well my garments sit upon
    me.
My brother's servants were then my fellows, now they are
    my men.

Sebastian: But for your conscience?

Antonio: Ay, where lies that? Twenty consciences
Stand 'twixt me and Milan, **candied be they
And melt ere they molest.**
Here lies your brother, if he were dead;
Whom I, with this obedient steel – three inches of it –
Can lay to bed forever.
The rest'll take suggestion as a cat laps milk.

they'll turn into crystals and dissolve before they interfere

Sebastian: As thou got'st Milan, I'll come by Naples.
Draw thy sword, and I the king shall love thee.

Antonio: Draw together.

Sebastian: One word.
*(He takes Antonio aside to talk. Enter Ariel with music and
    song.)*

Ariel: My master through his art foresees the danger
And sends me forth to keep them living.
(Ariel sings in Gonzalo's ear)
Awake, awake!

Gonzalo: *(Waking)* Preserve the King!

Alonso: Why are you drawn?

Why have you drawn your swords?

Gonzalo: What's the matter?

Sebastian: Whiles we stood here securing your repose,
We heard bellowing like bulls or lions.

Alonso: Heard you this, Gonzalo?

Gonzalo: I heard a humming, which did awake me.
I shaked you, sir, and cried. As mine eyes opened,
I saw their weapons drawn.
'Tis best we stand upon our guard,
Or that we quit this place. Let's draw our weapons.

Alonso: Lead off this ground, and let's make further search
For my poor son.

> ## Think about it
>
> What do you think Sebastian says to Antonio when he takes him aside?

23

Caliban meets two more survivors, discovers alcohol and makes a friend!

All the infections that the sun sucks up from bogs, fens, flats, on Prosper fall, and make him by inchmeal a disease!

Here comes a spirit of his, and to torment me for bringing wood in slowly. I'll fall flat; perchance he will not **mind** me.

Another storm brewing. If it should thunder as it did before, I know not where to hide my head.

What have we here? He smells like a fish. Warm! This is no fish, but an islander that hath suffered by a thunderbolt.

The storm is come again. My best way is to creep under his **gaberdine** till the storm be past.

mind – notice
gaberdine – cloak

He's in his fit now. – He's panicking.

Four legs and two voices - a most delicate monster!

Stephano, speak to me, for I am thy good friend Trinculo.

I'll pull thee by the legs.

Thou art Trinculo indeed!

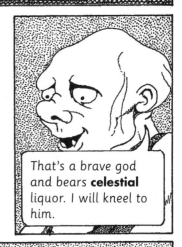

That's a brave god and bears **celestial** liquor. I will kneel to him.

How cam'st thou hither? I escaped upon a **butt of sack**.

Swum ashore, man, like a duck.

Hast any more of this?

In a rock by th' sea-side.

Hast thou not dropped from heaven?

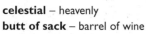

celestial – heavenly
butt of sack – barrel of wine

I was the man i' th' moon.

I do adore thee.

Come, **kiss the book**. I will furnish it anon with new contents.

I'll show thee every inch o' th' island. I will kiss thy foot. I prithee, be my god.

The poor monster's in drink.

I'll show thee the best springs; I'll pluck berries; I'll fish and get wood. A plague upon the tyrant that I serve! I'll bear him no more sticks but follow thee.

A most ridiculous monster – to make a wonder of a poor drunkard!

'Ban, 'ban, Ca-caliban, has a new master, get a new man.

Lead the way.

kiss the book – have another drink

27

Prospero makes Ferdinand work hard! This upsets Miranda, who has fallen in love with the young man.

I must remove some thousands of these logs and pile them up. My sweet mistress weeps when she sees me work.

But these sweet thoughts do even refresh my labours.

Work not so hard. My father is hard at study; rest yourself. He's safe for these three hours.

Give me that; I'll carry it to the pile.

No, I had rather break my back than you should such dishonour undergo.

Poor worm, **thou art infected**!

thou art infected – you're in love

**Act 3
Scene 1**

Ferdinand tells Miranda that he loves
her and they plan to get married.

Miranda: You look wearily.

Ferdinand: No, noble mistress, 'tis fresh morning with me
When you are by at night. I do beseech you –
Chiefly that I might set it in my prayers –
What is your name?

Miranda: Miranda. – O my father,
I have **broke your hest** to say so!   disobeyed your command

Ferdinand: Full many a lady I have eyed with best regard.
For several virtues
Have I liked several women; never any
With so full soul, but some defect in her
Did quarrel with the noblest grace she owed
And **put it to the foil**. But you, O you,   defeated it
So perfect and so peerless, are created
Of every creature's best.

Miranda: I do not know one of my sex. Nor have I seen
More that I may call men than you, good friend,
And my dear father. I would not wish
Any companion in the world but you,
Nor can imagination form a shape
Besides yourself, to like of.

Ferdinand: I am a prince, Miranda.
The very instant that I saw you, did
My heart fly to your service, there resides
To make me slave to it, and for your sake
Am I this patient log-man.

Miranda: Do you love me?

Ferdinand: I do love, prize, honour you.

Miranda: I am a fool to weep at what I am glad of.

Prospero: *(Aside)* Heavens rain grace on that which
   breeds between 'em.

Ferdinand: Wherefore weep you?

Miranda: At mine unworthiness that dare not offer
What I desire to give; and much less take
What I shall die to want.
I am your wife, if you will marry me;
If not, I'll die your maid. To be your fellow
You may deny me, but I'll be your servant
Whether you will or no.

Ferdinand: My mistress, dearest, and I thus humble ever.

Miranda: My husband, then?

Ferdinand: Ay, with a heart as willing
As bondage e'er of freedom. Here's my hand.

Miranda: And mine, with my heart in't. And now
   farewell
Till half an hour hence.

                              (They leave)

Prospero: So glad of this as they I cannot be,
Who are surprised withal, but my rejoicing
At nothing can be more.

Think about it

Why do you think Miranda and Ferdinand
fall for each other so quickly?

Act 3 Scene 2

Caliban wants Stephano to kill Prospero. Ariel causes a fight by imitating Trinculo's voice.

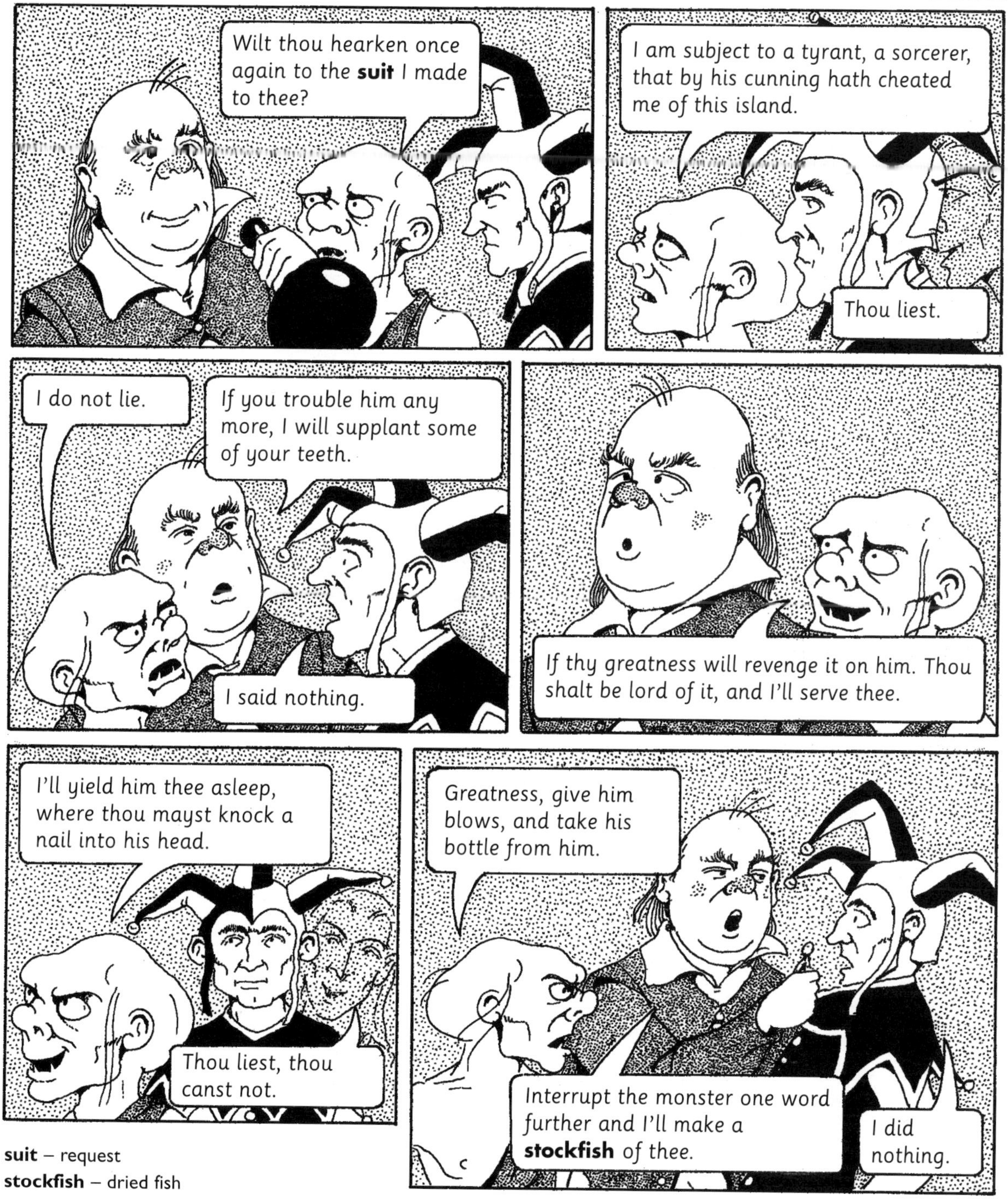

Wilt thou hearken once again to the **suit** I made to thee?
I am subject to a tyrant, a sorcerer, that by his cunning hath cheated me of this island.
Thou liest.
I do not lie.
If you trouble him any more, I will supplant some of your teeth.
I said nothing.
If thy greatness will revenge it on him. Thou shalt be lord of it, and I'll serve thee.
I'll yield him thee asleep, where thou mayst knock a nail into his head.
Thou liest, thou canst not.
Greatness, give him blows, and take his bottle from him.
Interrupt the monster one word further and I'll make a **stockfish** of thee.
I did nothing.

suit – request
stockfish – dried fish

paunch – stab (in the stomach)
wezand – windpipe (throat)   **sot** – drunken fool

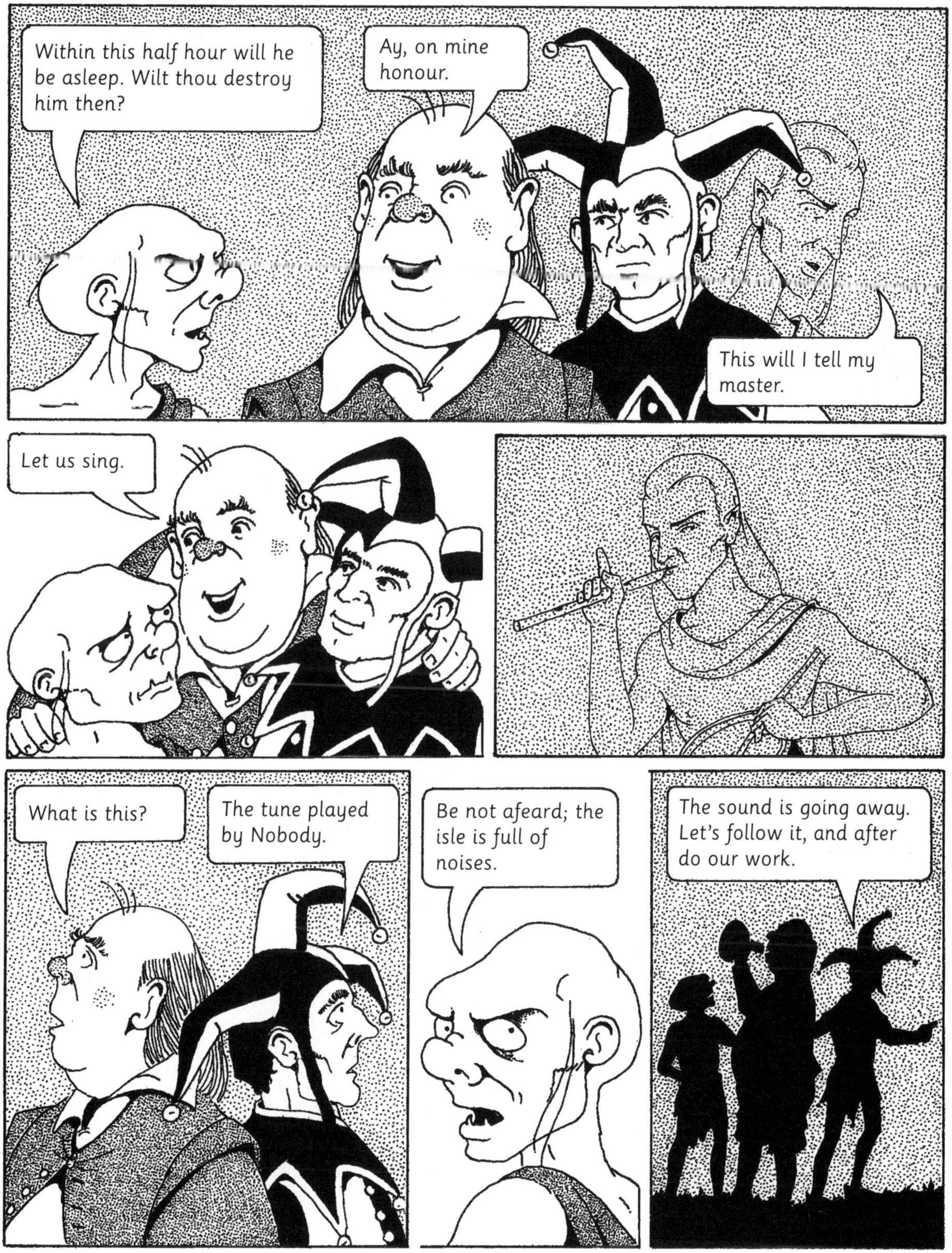
Within this half hour will he be asleep. Wilt thou destroy him then?
Ay, on mine honour.
This will I tell my master.
Let us sing.
What is this?
The tune played by Nobody.
Be not afeard; the isle is full of noises.
The sound is going away. Let's follow it, and after do our work.

Prospero works his magic to confuse and punish Alonso and the other noblemen.

repulse – failed attempt

What **harmony** is this? What were these?

If in Naples I should report this now, would they believe me? Yet their manners are more gentle than of our human generation you shall find many.

Honest lord, thou hast said well, for some of you there present are worse than devils.

They vanished strangely!

No matter, since they have left their **viands** behind. Will't please you to taste of what is here?

I will stand to and feed, although my last; no matter, since I feel the best is past.

harmony – entertainment
viands – food

You are three men of sin. I have made you mad.

You three from Milan did supplant good Prospero, exposed unto the sea, which hath **requit** it, him and his innocent child; the powers have **incensed** the seas and shores against your peace.

Thee of thy son, Alonso, they have bereft, and do pronounce by me **ling'ring perdition**, worse than any death can be at once, shall step by step attend you and your ways.

requit – repaid   **incensed** – angered
ling'ring perdition – everlasting ruin

these fits – their confusion   it did bass my trespass – it spoke of my crime in a loud, deep voice
ecstasy – madness

**Act 4
Scene 1**

Prospero agrees to the marriage. He
calls spirits to bless the couple before
using Ariel to deal with Caliban.

Prospero: If I have too **austerely** punished you,   severely
Your compensation makes amends, for I
Have given you here a third of mine own life,
Or that for which I live, who once again
I tender to thy hand. All thy vexations
Were but my trials of thy love, and thou
Hast strangely stood the test. Here, afore heaven,
I **ratify** this my rich gift. O Ferdinand,   confirm
Do not smile at me that I boast her off,
For thou shalt find she will outstrip all praise
And make it halt behind her.

Ferdinand: I do believe it against an oracle.

Prospero: Then, as my gift and thine own acquisition,
Worthily purchased, take my daughter. But
If thou dost break her virgin-knot before
All **sanctimonious** ceremonies may   holy
With full and holy rite be ministered,
No sweet **aspersion** shall the heavens let fall   shower (of holy water)
To make this contract grow; but barren hate,
Sour-eyed disdain and discord shall bestrew
The union of your bed with weeds so loathly
That you shall hate it both. Therefore take heed,
As **Hymen's** lamps shall light you.   the god of marriage

Ferdinand: I hope for quiet days, fair **issue**, and long life,   children
With such love as 'tis now, the murkiest den,
The most opportune place, the strong'st suggestion
Our worser genius can, shall never melt
Mine honour into lust to take away
The edge of that day's celebration
When I shall think or **Phoebus' steeds** are foundered   the god of the sun   horses
Or night kept chained below.

38

Prospero: Fairly spoke.
Sit then and talk with her; she is thine own.
What, Ariel! My industrious servant, Ariel!

(Enter Ariel)

Ariel: What would my potent master? Here I am.

Prospero: I must use you in another trick. Go bring the
  rabble   Ariel's spirit servants
(O'er whom I give thee power) here to this place.
Incite them to quick motion, for I must   Make them hurry
Bestow upon the eyes of this young couple
Some vanity of mine art. It is my promise,
And they expect it from me.

Ariel: Before you can say 'come' and 'go',
Each one will be here.

Prospero: Do not approach till thou dost hear me call.
  (To Ferdinand)
Look thou be true. Do not give **dalliance**   love-making
Too much the rein. The strongest oaths are straw
To th' fire i' th' blood. Be more abstemious
Or else good night your vow!

Ferdinand: I warrant you, sir,
The white cold virgin snow upon my heart
Abates the ardour of my liver.

Prospero: No tongue, all eyes. Be silent!

Think about it

Why does Prospero threaten Ferdinand in this way?

Ceres, most bounteous lady, the **queen o' th' sky**, whose **watery arch** and messenger am I, bids thee leave and with her sovereign grace, here on this grass-plot, in this very place, to come and sport.

Approach, rich Ceres, her to entertain.

Why hath thy queen summoned me to this short-grassed green?

A contract of true love to celebrate.

queen o' th' sky – Juno
watery arch – rainbow

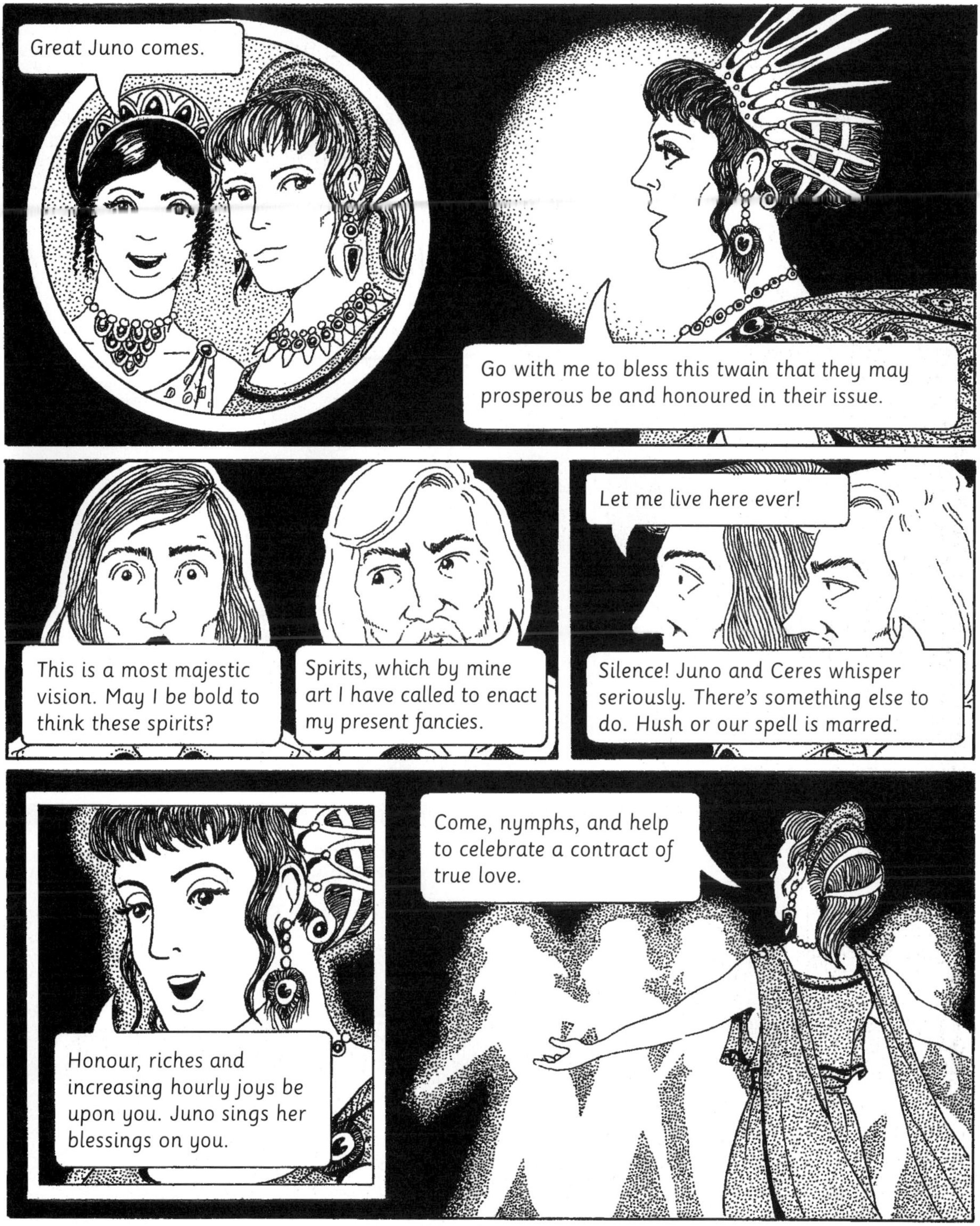
Great Juno comes.
Go with me to bless this twain that they may prosperous be and honoured in their issue.
This is a most majestic vision. May I be bold to think these spirits?
Spirits, which by mine art I have called to enact my present fancies.
Let me live here ever!
Silence! Juno and Ceres whisper seriously. There's something else to do. Hush or our spell is marred.
Honour, riches and increasing hourly joys be upon you. Juno sings her blessings on you.
Come, nymphs, and help to celebrate a contract of true love.

I had forgot that foul conspiracy of the beast Caliban and his confederates against my life. The minute of their plot is almost come.

Well done. **Avoid**, no more.

This is strange. Your father's in some passion.

Never till this day saw I him touched with anger so distempered!

Our revels now are ended. These spirits are melted into thin air, like the great globe itself, all shall dissolve. We are such stuff as dreams are made on, and our little life is **rounded** with a sleep.

Bear with my weakness, my old brain is troubled. Retire into my cell, and there repose. A turn or two I'll walk to still my beating mind.

We wish your peace.

Ariel. Come!

What's thy pleasure?

We must prepare to meet with Caliban.

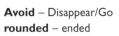

Avoid – Disappear/Go
rounded – ended

42

varlets – villains   **filthy-mantled** – slime-covered

trumpery – fancy clothes   **stale** – bait

on whose nature nurture can never stick – whose character can never be changed

Do that good mischief which may make this island thine own forever, and I, thy Caliban, for aye thy foot-licker.

I do begin to have bloody thoughts.

O King Stephano! Look what a wardrobe here is for thee!

Let it alone, thou fool; it is but trash.

I'll have that gown.

Thy grace shall have it.

Let't alone and do the murder first.

If he be awake, he'll fill our skins with pinches, make us strange stuff.

Be quiet, monster.

Put some **lime** upon your fingers, and away with the rest.

I'll have none on't. We shall lose time.

Help to bear this away; carry this.

And this.

lime – bird-lime (a type of glue)

Go, charge my goblins that they may grind their joints with dry convulsions, shorten up their sinews with aged cramps, and more pinch-spotted make them than **pard or cat o' mountain**.

Hark, they roar!

Let them be hunted. At this hour lies at my mercy all mine enemies. Shortly shall all my labours end, and thou shalt have the air at freedom. For a little, follow and do me service.

pard or cat o'mountain – leopard or panther

**Act 5
Scene 1**

Prospero traps the noblemen in a magic circle and plans to tell them his true identity.

Now does my project gather to a head.

How's the day?

On the sixth hour, at which time, my lord, you said our work should cease.

I did say so, when first I raised the tempest.

How fares the King and's followers?

All prisoners, sir, in the **line-grove**.

Go, release them, Ariel. My charms I'll break; their senses I'll restore; and they shall be themselves.

This rough magic I here **abdure** ...

... and when I have required some heavenly music to work mine end upon their senses, I'll break my staff, bury it certain **fathoms** in the earth, and deeper than did ever **plummet** sound I'll drown my book.

line-grove – lime trees   **abdure** – renounce/give up
fathoms – a measurement of depth (1 fathom = 1.8m)   **plummet** – a weight on a rope used to measure the sea's depth

There stand, for you are spell-stopped.

Ariel, fetch me the hat and rapier in my cell. I will **discase me**, and myself present as I was sometime Milan.

discase me – get changed

Ariel! I shall miss thee, but yet thou shalt have freedom.

To the King's ship; there shalt thou find the mariners asleep. Enforce them to this place.

Gonzalo: All torment, trouble, wonder and amazement
Inhabits here. Some heavenly power guide us
Out of this fearful country.

Prospero: Behold, sir King,
The wronged Duke of Milan, Prospero!
To thee and thy company I bid
A hearty welcome.

Alonso: Whe'er thou be'st he or no,
Or some enchanted trifle to abuse me,
(As late I have been), I know not. Thy pulse
Beats as of flesh and blood; and since I saw thee,
Th'affliction of my mind amends, with which
I fear a madness held me.
This must crave a most strange story.
Thy dukedom I resign and do entreat
Thou pardon me my wrongs. But how should Prospero
Be living, and be here?

Prospero: *(To Gonzalo)*   First, noble friend,
Let me embrace thine age, whose honour cannot
Be measured or confined.

Gonzalo: Whether this be, or be not, I'll not swear.

Prospero: Welcome, my friends all.
(To Sebastian and Antonio)   But you, my lords,
Were I so minded, I could justify you traitors!
At this time I will tell no tales.

Sebastian: The devil speaks in him.

Prospero: No. For you, most wicked sir, whom to call
     brother
Would even infect my mouth, I do forgive
Thy rankest fault – all of them; and require
My dukedom of thee, which perforce I know
Thou must restore.

Alonso: If thou be'st Prospero,
Give us particulars of thy preservation,
How thou hast met us here, whom three hours since
Were wrecked upon this shore, where I have lost
My dear son Ferdinand.
Irreparable is the loss, and patience
Says it is past her cure.

Prospero: I rather think
You have not sought her help, of whose soft grace
For the like loss I have her sovereign aid
And rest myself content.

Alonso: You the like loss?

Prospero: As great to me as late; and supportable
To make the dear loss, have I means much weaker
Than you may call to comfort you, for I
Have lost my daughter.

Alonso: A daughter?
O heavens, that they were living both in Naples,
The king and queen there! That they were, I wish
Myself were mudded in that oozy bed
Where my son lies. When did you lose your daughter?

Prospero: In this last tempest. – I perceive these lords
At this encounter do so much admire
That they devour their reason and **scarce think**
Their eyes do offices of truth, their words
Are natural breath. – But howsoe'er you have
Been jostled from your senses, know for certain
That I am Prospero, and that very duke
Who most strangely upon this shore was landed.
No more yet of this,
For 'tis a chronicle of day by day,
Not a **relation** for a breakfast, nor
Befitting this first meeting. – Welcome, sir;
This cell's my court; here have I few attendants,
And subjects none abroad.

> **Think about it**
>
> Why do Alonso and Gonzalo doubt the evidence of their eyes when they see Prospero?

don't believe what they see

report/story

Prospero brings Alonso and Ferdinand together and the ship's crew is released from the spell.

Pray you, look in.

Sweet lord, you play me false.

No, my dearest love, not for the world.

If this prove a **vision** of the island, one dear son shall I twice lose.

A most high miracle!

Though the seas threaten, they are merciful. I have cursed them without cause.

vision — illusion/trick

How many goodly creatures are there here!

O brave new world that has such people in't.

'Tis new to thee.

What is this maid with whom thou wast at play? Is she the goddess that hath **severed** us and brought us thus together?

Sir, she is mortal; but she's mine.

She is daughter to this famous Duke of Milan.

Look down, you gods, and on this couple drop a blessed crown.

I say 'amen', Gonzalo.

severed – parted

In one voyage did Claribel her husband find at Tunis, and Ferdinand, her brother, found a wife, where he himself was lost, Prospero his dukedom in a poor isle, and all of us ourselves, when no man was his own.

Look, sir, here is more of us.

What is the news?

The best news is that we have safely found our king and company.

Our ship is **tight and yare**, and bravely rigged as when we first put out to sea.

Sir, all this service have I done since I went.

My **tricksy** spirit!

tight and yare – shipshape/seaworthy
tricksy – clever/cunning

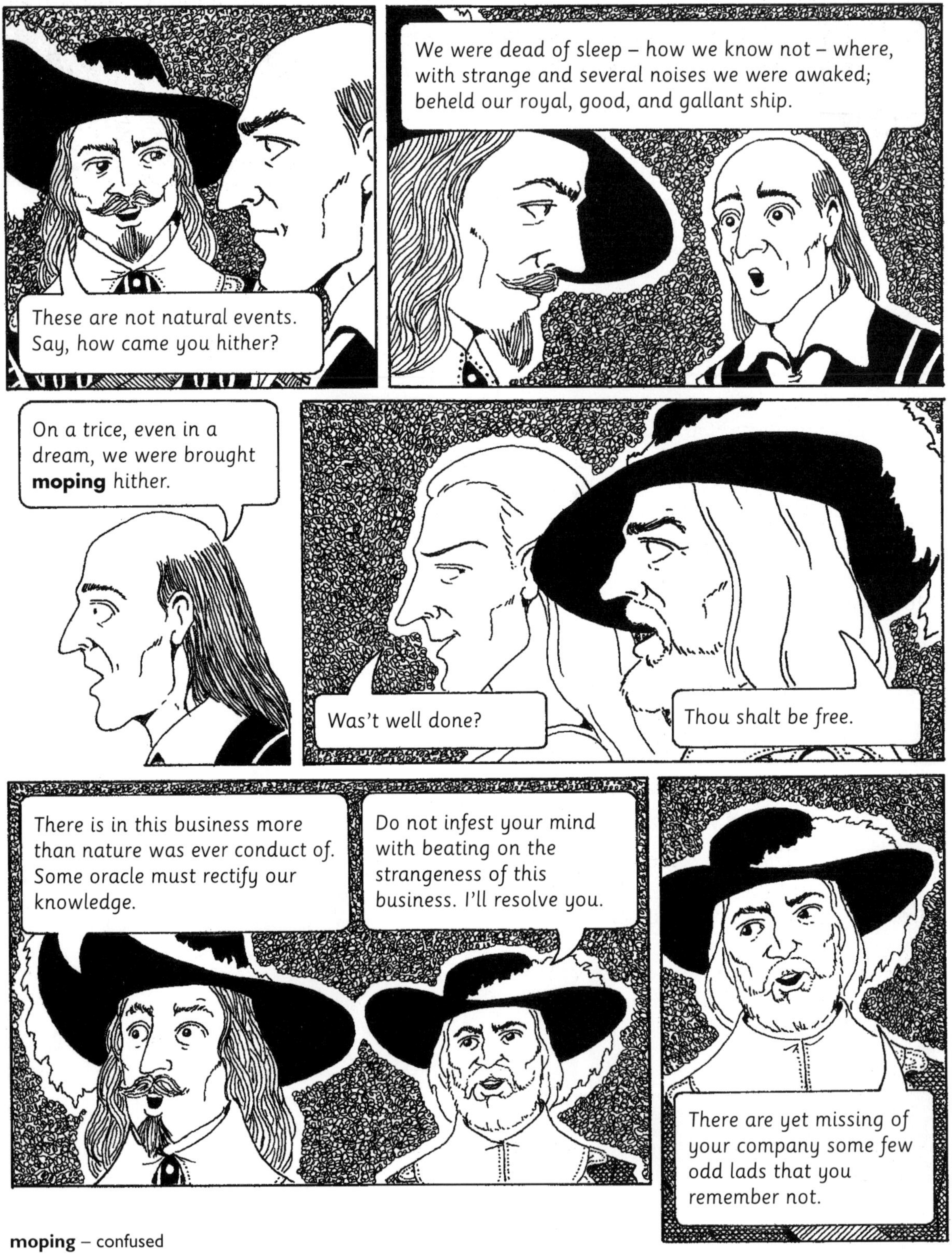
These are not natural events. Say, how came you hither?
We were dead of sleep – how we know not – where, with strange and several noises we were awaked; beheld our royal, good, and gallant ship.
On a trice, even in a dream, we were brought **moping** hither.
Was't well done?
Thou shalt be free.
There is in this business more than nature was ever conduct of. Some oracle must rectify our knowledge.
Do not infest your mind with beating on the strangeness of this business. I'll resolve you.
There are yet missing of your company some few odd lads that you remember not.

moping – confused

<table>
<tr><td>

**Act 5
Scene 1**

</td><td>

Caliban is dealt with and Prospero will tell his story before they return to Naples. Ariel is given his freedom.

</td><td>

</td></tr>
</table>

Sebastian: What things are these, my lord Antonio?
Will money buy 'em?

Antonio: Very like. One of them
Is a plain fish and no doubt marketable.

Prospero: Mark but the badges of these men, my lords,
Then say if they be true. This misshapen knave,
His mother was a witch, and one so strong
That could control the moon, make flows and ebbs,
And deal in her command without her power.
These three have robbed me, and this demi-devil
(For he's a bastard one) had plotted with them
To take my life. Two of these fellows you
Must know and own; this thing of darkness I
Acknowledge mine.

Caliban: I shall be pinched to death.

Alonso: Is not this Stephano, my drunken butler?

Sebastian: He is drunk now. Where had he wine?

Alonso: And Trinculo is reeling ripe! Where should they
Find this grand liquor that hath gilded 'em?
How cam'st thou in this pickle?

Trinculo: I have been in such a pickle since I saw you last that I fear me will never out of my bones. I shall not fear **fly-blowing**.   flies laying their eggs (on me)

Sebastian: Why, how now, Stephano?

Stephano: O touch me not; I am not Stephano, but a cramp.

Prospero: You'd be king o' th' isle, **sirrah**?   sir

55

Stephano: I should have been a sore one then.

Alonso: This is a strange thing as e'er I looked on.

Prospero: He is as disproportioned in his manners
As in his shape. Go to my cell;
Take with you your companions. As you look
To have my pardon, **trim** it handsomely.   decorate

Caliban: Ay, that I will; and I'll be wise hereafter
And seek for grace. What a thrice-double ass
Was I to take this drunkard for a god,
And worship this dull fool!

Prospero: Go to, away.

Alonso: Bestow **your luggage** where you found it.   the stolen clothes

Sebastian: Or stole it rather.

Think about it

Why does Caliban
apologize? What might
happen to him now?

Sir, I invite your highness and your **train** to my poor cell, where you shall take your rest for this one night …

… which (part of it) I'll waste with such **discourse** as, I not doubt, shall make it go quick away – the story of my life and the particular accidents gone by since I came to this isle.

In the morn I'll bring you to your ship, and so to Naples, where I have hope to see the **nuptial** of these our dear-beloved solemnized; and thence retire me to my Milan, where every third thought shall be my grave.

I long to hear the story of your life.

I'll deliver all, and promise you calm seas.

My Ariel. That is thy charge. Then to the elements be free and fare thou well!

train – followers   **discourse** – talk
nuptial – marriage

Now my charms are all o'erthrown,
And what strength I have's mine own,
Which is most faint. Now, 'tis true
I must be here confined by **you**,
Or sent to Naples. Let me not,
Since I have my dukedom got
And pardoned the deceiver, dwell
In this bare island by your spell;
But release me from my bands
With the help of your **good hands**.
Gentle breath of yours my sails
Must fill, or else my project fails,
Which was to please. Now I **want**
Spirits to enforce, art to enchant;
And my ending is despair,
Unless I be relieved by prayer,
Which pierces so that it assaults
Mercy itself, and frees all faults.
    As you from crimes would pardoned be,
    Let your indulgence set me free.

The end

you – the audience   **good hands** – applause   **want** – lack